PENGUIN BOOKS

THE PENGUIN BOOK
OF INDIAN CARTOONS

Abu Abraham was born in Tiruvalla, Kerala, in 1924. He studied
Mathematics, English and French at Kerala University and obtained a
B.Sc degree in 1945. His first job as a journalist was at the *Bombay
Chronicle* (1946-49). Later he worked for a couple of years with
Shankar's Weekly in New Delhi before joining the *Observer* in England as staff cartoonist in 1956. He worked with that newspaper for 10
years and then did a three-year stint with the *Guardian* which described
him as the most original among Europe's post-war cartoonists. The
Guardian said of him, 'Abu is the conscience of the Left and pea under
the princess's mattress. His drawings are the reading between the lines,
the uncomfortably direct reminder that after all the weighing of expe-
diencies, politics is concerned with moral questions.'

Abu Abraham is the author of several books including *Abu on Ban-
gladesh, Private View, Games of Emergency* and *Arrivals and Depar-
tures*. He has also edited a collection of cartoons from all over the
world on the Vietnam war, *Verdicts on Vietnam*. He was given a special
award by the British Film Institute in 1970 for his animated cartoon
film *No Arks*.

Mr. Abraham was nominated a member of the Rajya Sabha, the
Upper House of the Indian Parliament (1972-78).

Abu Abraham lives in New Delhi.

D1157456

THE PENGUIN BOOK OF

INDIAN CARTOONS

Selected and Introduced by
ABU ABRAHAM

PENGUIN BOOKS

Penguin Books India (P) Ltd., B4/246 Safdarjung Enclave, New Delhi-110029, India
Penguin Books Ltd., 27 Wrights Lane, London W8 5TZ, U.K.
Penguin Books USA Inc., 375 Hudson Street, New York, N.Y., 10014, USA
Penguin Books Australia Ltd., Ringwood, Victoria, Australia
Penguin Books Canada Ltd., 10 Alcorn Avenue, Suite 300, Toronto, Ontario M4V 3B2, Canada
Penguin Books (NZ) Ltd., 182-190 Wairu Road, Auckland 10, New Zealand

First published by Penguin Books 1988
Reprinted 1988, 1989, 1991, 1992

Pages VII, IX & X constitute an extension to the copyright page.
Made and printed in India by Ananda Offset Private Limited, Calcutta.
Typeset in Times Roman

To my sister, Ammu,
whose laughter I miss.

ACKNOWLEDGEMENTS

I express my sincere thanks here to all the cartoonists who have shown interest in this volume and have lent their cooperation, and to their newspapers and magazines (listed on page IX & X) for permission to reproduce these cartoons. The Birla Academy of Art and Culture in Calcutta graciously allowed the reproduction of the drawings of Gogonendranath Tagore in the preface. While every effort has been made to contact copyright holders, the publishers would be interested to hear from copyright holders who remain unacknowledged. I would like to thank Krishna Swamy who took care of all the secretarial work involved and helped me with the selection. Finally, I am grateful to Psyche Chatterji and Ayisha Abraham for their careful scrutiny and advice during the arrangement of these cartoons.

LIST OF CARTOONISTS
IN ORDER OF APPEARANCE

Most of the cartoonists included in this volume work for newspapers or magazines. The publications they work for are placed next to their names in parentheses. Their noms de plume are in bold.

Vikram Verma (Civil and Military Gazette)
Vasu (Pioneer)
K **Shankar** Pillai (Shankar's Weekly)
Abu Abraham (Shankar's Weekly, Sunday Observer, Patriot, Tribune, The Telegraph)
Ravi Shankar (Indian Express)
P.K.S.**Kutty** (Hindustan Standard, Shankar's Weekly)
Enver **Ahmed** (Hindusthan Times)
Raobail (The Daily)
R.K. Laxman (Times of India)
Murthy—B.V. Ramamurthy (Deccan Herald)
B.M.**Geffoor** (Mathrubhoomi)
Vishnu Sharma (Shankar's Weekly)
Mohan Sivanand (Science Today, Mid-Day)
Sudhir Dar (Hindustan Times)
Dizi (Shankar's Weekly)
Rajinder **Puri** (Statesman, Tribune)
Manik (Diwana)
Bagga (Hindustan Times)
Mario Miranda (Illustrated Weekly of India, Economic Times)
Jaspal Bhatti (Tribune)
Manohar **Sapre** (Hitavada)
Kevy-Kerala Varma (Eastern Economist)
Unny (The Hindu)
Kanti (Shankar's Weekly)
Negi (Shankar's Weekly)
Ravi (Ananda Vikatan)
Vins-Vijay N. Seth (Mid-Day)
Mickey Patel (Patriot)
Ajit **Ninan** (India Today)

Prakash Ghosh (Shankar's Weekly)
Vani—K.V. Ramani (Ananda Vikatan)
C.J. Yesudasan (The Week)
Jar (Times of India)
Babu (Malayala Manorama)
Vivek (Ananda Vikatan)
Mandoo (Shankar's Weekly)
Amal Chakrabarti (Amrita Bazar Patrika)
Manjula Padmanabhan (Sunday Observer, Freedom First)
N.S. **Ponnappa** (Deccan Herald, Reader's Digest, Architecture and Design)
Kaak (Navbharat Times)
Ashwath—Aswathanarayana (Aparanji)
Him-Himanish Goswami (Amrita Bazar Patrika)
Hemant K. **Morparia** (Illustrated Weekly of India)
O.V. **Vijayan** (The Statesman)
Sudarsan (Ananda Vikatan)
Madhan (Ananda Vikatan)
Gopi Gajwani (Destination India, American Centre Publications)
Ramakrishna (Shankar's Weekly)
Sudhir Tailang (Navbharat Times)
Kesi—Keshav (Ananda Vikatan)
Rajini Shetty (Hindustan Times)
Ranga (The Statesman)
G. **Aravindan** (Mathrubhoomi)

INTRODUCTION

While the decline of political wit is a recurrent subject of discussion in Britain and America, a frequent topic of our times in India is the virtual absence of wit in public life. Indeed, the Indian intelligentsia never seem to tire of saying that Indians have no sense of humour.

This is a sweeping assertion and, in my view, an ignorant one too. It is possible that they are talking about themselves or their social milieu. A certain type of English-educated Indian, who is most likely to have been to a 'public' or Mission school, and has been taught to emulate the mores of the British and other such dominant peoples, tends to make an ass of himself when trying to be witty in a foreign language. He may be a *pucca sahib* in every other way, but his 'wit' can be quite appalling.

The common people (especially the rural), on the other hand, have a way of laughing at their own misfortunes. They can also laugh at their oppressors. Satire became a habit with them while they groaned under the oppression of kings, priests and plutocrats. In contemporary India, the politician and the bureaucrat are the ones they take their revenge upon.

There is much humour in Indian proverbs. Even the gods are not spared. There is a special form of worship called *ninda-stuti,* praise by dispraise.

Real humour in India, as elsewhere, is contained within the different languages and it is as difficult for Indians of one region to understand the humour of another, as it is for the English-educated Indian to absorb the true flavour of English humour. India is also by tradition a class-ridden and hierarchical society. Excessive reverence is shown to elders and to those in authority, though this may be changing. Sons and daughters don't usually joke with their parents and vice-versa; a boss can't afford to be seen in a mood of levity with his employees; the landlord wouldn't dream of sharing a joke with his peasant labourers. The path to wit and humour is strewn with pitfalls.

With Indian intellectuals, solemnity is a motto. Many of them wouldn't be seen dead with a joke. And the higher they go in the cerebral scale, the drier they become. 'All jokes are schoolboyish,' said the editor of a national daily to me once, though even his paper devotes the occasional 'third leader' to an effort at humour. Another national daily from the culturally traditional South similarly reserves a place for humour in a tucked-away corner on Sundays. This newspaper, when it started to publish the Art Buchwald column some years ago, placed this 'statutory warning' at the top: 'The following article is written in a humorous vein.'

It is a firm belief among Indian intellectuals and scholars that they will not be taken seriously if they are caught being witty. The phenomenon is not, of course, peculiar to India. It is by now well established that Adlai Stevenson lost the Presidential election (not once but twice) because of his irrepressible wit. And after seeing the political failure of such a good man American politicians seem to have, despite occasional lapses, taken to the well-known advice given by Senator Thomas Corwin to Garfield: 'Never make people laugh. If you would succeed in life, you must be solemn, solemn as an ass. All great monuments are built on solemn asses.'

Stevenson once spoke of the efficacy of humour in an interview with Leon Harris, author of *The Fine Art of Political Wit*. He said: 'I think it can be extremely effective, especially for Americans, because Americans are such sensible people, responsive to humour-ordinary Americans. I would hate to think that humour is, in the long run, more effective than reason, but it certainly is more arresting than reason. I think ridicule, and the best of us ridicule humorously, is effective where our political scene is concerned. Naturally I believe that reason must prevail. If it doesn't, we're lost. Humour is no substitute for reason. On the other hand, it certainly can illustrate and enrich reason.'

Stevenson comes close to a definition of the political cartoon. The best of them are indeed 'reason illustrated and enriched by humour'. Another definition could be derived from Aneurin Bevan's description of his own role in British Parliament. He once began a speech with these words: 'I welcome this opportunity of pricking the bloated bladder of lies with the poniard of truth.'

Bursting bloated bladders of lies or pomposity, cutting people down to size, these are the purposes of satire. The great masters of political wit of the past excelled in the subversive use of laughter. We no longer have men like Sheridan, Lloyd George, Winston Churchill and Aneurin Bevan on the British political scene. The nature of politics and administration has changed; this may be one reason. Also, there is too much work to be done in Parliament these days and there just isn't time for the leisurely after-dinner debates that once produced the sparks of malice that flashed across the chamber. Politics has become more gentlemanly. As the late Harold Macmillan remarked a few years ago, 'You can hardly say boo to a goose in the House of Commons now without cries of "Ungentlemanly", "Not fair", and all the rest.'

The output of wit and humour in the Indian Parliament has always been low. Neither in Hindi, the dominant language, nor in English, widely used on the floor as well as officially, has there been any memorable exchange of wit in the last four decades since India became free. But there have been political leaders who had a keen sense of humour, who could not only be witty but could enjoy wit at their own expense. Mahatma Gandhi was one such, and Sarojini Naidu and C. Rajagopalachari were two others. Gandhi's humour was gentle, though it could at times be barbed. When a foreign correspondent asked him what he thought of western civilization, Gandhi replied, 'It's a good idea.' Sarojini Naidu nicknamed Gandhi Mickey Mouse. If she had been able to draw, she would have made an excellent caricaturist. Nehru wasn't known for levity but he enjoyed wit and humour, and he could laugh at himself. He loved cartoons and collected many originals. Nehru, Gandhi and 'C.R.' were major actors on the cartoon stage of the time. In more recent times a truly witty performer in the Indian Parliament was the late Piloo Mody. He never missed a chance to provide comic relief in the House. His huge physical presence alone could manage that and he could claim, like Falstaff, 'I am not only witty in myself but the cause that wit is in other men.'

Both Nehru and his daughter, Indira Gandhi, enjoyed cartoons and considered them a necessary and useful institution in an otherwise pompous and self-centred world of politics. 'It's good to have the veil of our conceit torn occasionally' Nehru once said, referring to the veteran cartoonist, Shankar, who had been lampooning those in authority from well before the country's independence, until a decade ago, when he decided to retire from the political scene. Nehru's personal exhortation to Shankar, which he publicly expressed, was 'Don't spare me.'

There was a bleak period for cartoons and cartoonists during the Emergency (1975-77), when Mrs. Gandhi's government imposed pre-censorship on the press. But pre-censorship was lifted for cartoons after the first three months. I presume that this was done in order to relieve the boredom that had enveloped the press as well as politics.

'A thing that cannot stand laughter is not a good thing,' James Thurber once said. And an Emergency that could not take some ridicule couldn't be considered good either. Mrs. Gandhi acted wisely in letting cartoonists have their way.

Cartoonists everywhere have been a privileged lot. This is not only because they are a preciously rare breed among journalists but even more due to the fact that it is virtually impossible to edit cartoons. A cartoon is a total statement, which the editor (or reader) has either to take as it is or reject entirely. The blue pencil is of little value when dealing with a cartoon.

Cartooning, nevertheless, can be a dangerous profession. This was recently illustrated by what happened to the editor of *Ananda Vikatan,* a popular Tamil weekly magazine of Madras. The magazine published a cartoon showing two characters on a public platform, one supposed to be a member of the Tamil Nadu Assembly and looking like a pickpocket, and the other meant to be a minister resembling a dacoit. The idea was spelt out in so many words (in the caption). The Assembly Speaker, like the majority of the MLA's, was not amused and sentenced the editor Mr. Balasubramanian (who refused to apologize) to three months in prison. The event sent shock waves through the country and the press almost unanimously deplored the Speaker's action... though it was generally accepted that the cartoon as such was in poor taste. As it happened, the editor was released after a mere three days.

But cartoonists do manage to have their say even when their cartoons are an embarrassment to those in power. Helen Vlachos, the Greek newspaper owner, came to appreciate this while she was in exile during the rule of the colonels in Greece. She felt that cartoonists were able, even under a dictatorship, to maintain some kind of opposition. The printed word was too precise, she said. In Greece, the very ambiguity of some of the cartoons published gave them the subversive element so essential to the nature of this art. While the colonels were too dense to get the message, the readers worked it out with subtle skill.

Yet, it must be emphasized that a free environment is essential for the proper functioning of cartoonists. Ideas of liberty can at times be smuggled through in a cartoon but liberty itself is a condition for a cartoonist's continued existence.

On the whole, I think India is a congenial place for cartoonists. It has its aberrations, political and social, but it has a base of tolerance that has sustained a democracy for nearly four decades. Certain inhibitions exist, nevertheless. Religious fervour often takes on menacing attitudes and discretion often becomes the better part of satire. Reaction appears from time to time in fundamentalist clothes, and cartoonists have to take cover. One can write against religion, promote atheism, but to use satire against a religious phenomenon, whatever that be, will be to risk a violent demonstration, no doubt led by a young and aspiring 'leader of the masses.'

David Low has recalled in his autobiography a meeting he had with Mahatma Gandhi. This was while Gandhi was in England for the Round Table Conference. The Mahatma remarked that Indians had a lively appreciation of satire and therefore Low might find it useful to spend some time in India. But Low didn't respond to the suggestion because only a short while before one of his cartoons published in the *Star,* a London evening newspaper, very nearly caused a bloody riot in faraway Calcutta. Low had made the indiscretion of drawing the prophet (along with a number of other historical celebrities) in a rather facetious cartoon about the cricketer Jack Hobbs' batting record in some test match or the other.

Despite all these inhibitions — the distaste for humour for which Indian intellectuals are well-known, the nervous disposition of some of the editors and the explosive sensitivity of certain religious communities — cartooning has flourished in India and continues to do so. There is virtually no newspaper in the country that doesn't have a cartoonist or is not on the lookout for one. Even editors who may personally look down on anything approaching levity are happy to publish cartoons. This may be, I suppose, a case of the triumph of public opinion over editorial solemnity. When dealing with pompous editors, the circulation manager can be a cartoonist's ally.

Cartooning, like cricket, came to India with the British, whose arrival on these shores more or less coincided with the invention of the printing press. Both Indian journalism and Indian cartooning subsequently became, as British rule turned intolerable, vehicles of protest, agitation and peaceful revolution. Some of the viceroys and governors were keen collectors of originals depicting their own follies. That was the British way of showing that they had a sense of humour and that they admired the way the Indians had taken to the art of cartoons. As with cricket, cartoons created a bond between Britain and India.

It has been said that autocracy in France in the old days was tempered by epigram and in Russia by assassination; but in England oligarchy was tempered by caricature. Though the art, as we know it today, began in Italy and developed in France, Germany and Holland, it was in England that it became a popular and powerful medium of dissent and democratization of society. The cartoon in India today plays the same role. Cartoonists put down the mighty and exalt the lowly. And they provide humour and wit in a political and social environment where these are not plentiful.

A curious feature of cartooning in India is the disproportionately large number of its leading practitioners who come from the small southern state of Kerala. High literacy and (until recently) miserable poverty could be one of the reasons for this phenomenon. Kerala also has a long and rich tradition of satire in literature. The most famous of the satirical writers in Malayalam is Kunchan Nambiar who lived in the 18th century. The complete works of his hilarious writing, all in verse, make up a fat volume of more than 1200 pages. His barbs, always well-aimed, were directed at persons high and low, belonging to all classes and communities. And these verses are still a popular form of entertainment.

In Kerala, as well as in many other states, there are major concentrations of cartoonists. Literally hundreds practise the art, though only a few work at it full time. Most of these cartoonists have other more regular occupations like teaching, accountancy, law, medicine, the army or clerical work.

The cartoons in this volume are a personal selection, idiosyncratic in that they largely reflect my own tastes, though I have taken much advice from colleagues and friends. No book of this kind can either be complete or fully representative. Most of the cartoons are from the English language press. It couldn't be helped, since this volume is for an English-knowing public and often even the best translation cannot bring out the local flavour of captions. Besides, most of the drawings done in the regional papers are too regional in their themes.

I am glad to have been able to bring together these different talents, old and young, in a single volume. No such project was ever undertaken before in India. I am deeply grateful to all my colleagues in the profession for their warm and earnest cooperation.

Postscript:

I had decided to confine the scope of this book to the last fifty or so years of Indian cartooning. But I could not resist the temptation to include a couple of cartoons by Gaganendranath Tagore, a distinguished painter of an earlier period who also excelled in cartoons and caricatures. These are in the next two pages. Published in the 1920s, they satirize two familiar types, the anglicized Bengali and the rapacious priest. His style shows the influence of European masters of the art, like Phil May and Max Beerbohm.

Abu Abraham
New Delhi, July 1987.

The modern patriot

The temple priest sells his benediction

THE PENGUIN BOOK OF
INDIAN CARTOONS

Gandhiji with Viceroy Lord Linlithgow

ONE TOO MANY?

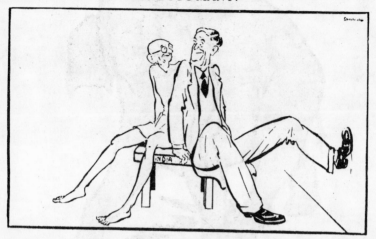

Mahatma Gandhi said "he and the Viceroy have come nearer each other" than ever before.

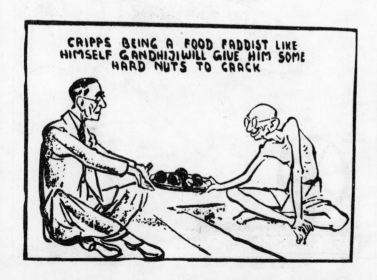

CRIPPS BEING A FOOD FADDIST LIKE HIMSELF GANDHIJI WILL GIVE HIM SOME HARD NUTS TO CRACK

SHANKAR

All this in his name!

One hundred years of solitude.

Jawaharlal Nehru

Birth of the sovereign republic: January 26, 1950

'Having come to understand there are vacancies in the Cabinet, I have the honour to apply…'

Nehru says public and private sectors must pull together.

The Congress is now to devote greater attention to rural uplift—Report.

The quality of mercy.

President Rajendra Prasad with Nehru

'*Rashtrapati Bhawan will be given an Indian look. We hope occupants and callers too!*'

R K LAXMAN

'You don't have to promise them anything, sir. This is not what has been declared famine area—it is further up!'

'*It's a pity that rainbearing clouds couldn't be brought under the Essential Commodities Act!*'

*'I wouldn't advise you to promise
drinking water. Promise something
simple.'*

*'You want water to drink? But
that's what the people of this
region have been demanding!'*

'*As there is no sea-coast within a thousand miles don't promise a harbour, sir!*'

'*The fact-finding team from Delhi having studied the drought situation in Kerala from Kovalam beach resort has reportedly stated that there is no water scarcity in the Arabian Sea.*'

'Rs.15/- crores loss here? Excellent. I thought everything
put together our village did not have more than Rs.50/-'

'What are you going to be when you grow up—illiterate, or
unemployed?'

'Now they have all gone! Must you start with that sort of
announcement ... "What you are about to see has no story,
no songs, no dance..."?'

'Had I secured employment in my younger days I'd
have educated you, and you'd now be an unemployed
graduate.'

'I'd like him to grow up, graduate, specialize in agriculture,
do post-doctoral research in high-yield grain hybrids, and
apply for permanent residence in the United States.'

'*That's no way to popularize science!*'

'*You don't have to come along, sir. We will attend to everything. We are actually qualified engineers*'

'Shame on you! Don't you know that we abolished
begging by an Act in the Assembly?'

R K LAXMAN

'I am delighted to note that your war on poverty has
produced such swift results…!'

'*Popcorn, chocolates, chewing gum,
potato chips, pills…*'

'The State Electricity Board plans
to electrify 1,000 more villages.
Family planning drive, I suppose.'

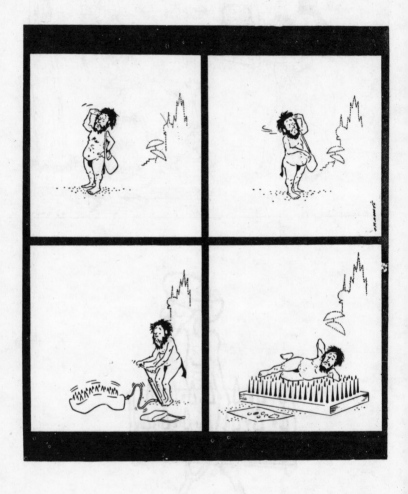

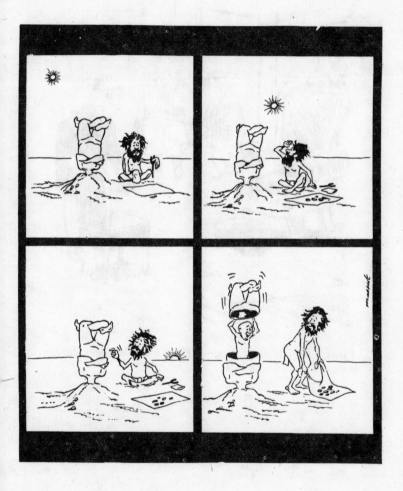

R K LAXMAN

'*Please take your seat, Your Highness, the Minister will be with you in a minute.*'

'I am more honest than you are. There are eight corruption charges against you and only six against me!'

Are we supposed to oppose corruption, or amend it?

'True, I have committed many blunders, irregularities, mistakes — but all in the interest of our country!'

'Same here; I am very popular outside my country, but inside my people don't understand me.'

But we have got to keep it here, sir, till the capital is paid. This was pledged as security!

R K LAXMAN

'We have a loan scheme; I assure you, it is equally good.
Why don't you try that instead?'

SUDHIR DAR

'Sahib is going on an indefinite fast from tomorrow!'

R K LAXMAN

'Thanks a lot—now I will tell you why I resigned from that party and why I want to rejoin the Congress.'

MARIO/MURTHY

'Don't you worry, it's only part of my salary, not my income.'

'In the Assembly today we raised our
pay so that we may not be accused of
living beyond our means!'

'I took 5 kilos of rice as a souvenir of the
glorious struggle of the masses for a fair
price. You call that looting?'

'So much of the stuff was available
and without a queue I couldn't
resist it! I wonder what it is.'

'The film which inspired me to commit
the crime had a happy ending!'

'Patients accustomed to adulterated
food respond only to spurious drugs!'

'I have discovered a cheaper
substitute for kerosene to
adulterate diesel with.'

'No Sir, an honest official will not
be suitable. This is a very
important post.'

'Postponed! All decisions postponed!'

'Where's the party, Daddy-O?'

'Certainly I'll join, but, by the
way, may I know what party?'

'I'm giving education just one more try... if I fail again,
I'm entering politics!'

ABU/SAPRE

'And now, will you please name the actor?'

'One of you is my son. I want him to come home with me!'

'Precocious boy, he gets the prize for writing on
workload reduction for teachers.'

'Yes, it is pretty unfair. They should allow free mid-day snacks for teachers too.'

'To save democracy, is it? I have been hurling stones
thinking it's about our teachers' pay!'

'You won't believe it Daddy, I took over as the
vice-chancellor today.'

'*When he shouted "paper, paper" I never thought he was selling question papers!*'

'He has started wearing tribal headgear in the hope that when the Prime Minister visits his State he might be able to meet him!'

'We can't sell you these drugs of ours until you get lung cancer from our cigarettes.'

'You've opened the wrong bag... this muck is for my customers.'

'No thanks, we know all about those classified carcinogenic additives.'

'An American art collector has bought his moustache.'

'Only one of my legs is on the footboard.
Will you charge me half fare?'

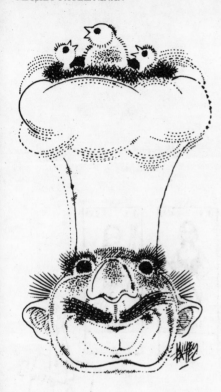

-Prakash

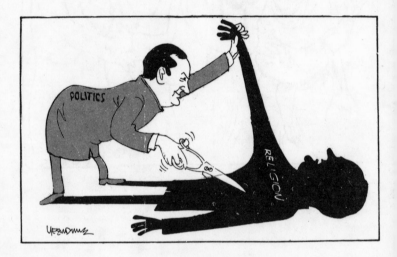

'We are impressed, but my son would like to know her other interests.'

I hereby solemnly affirm that Daddy will find me a well-placed (IAS or engineer) boy of wealthy parentage and refuse to offer dowry...

'He's a bank manager, wants five lakhs deposited before he will marry my daughter.'

'Oh no, not any more! You have got to find some other way to get rid of your unaccounted money !'

'The hi-fi equipment has been installed, and you will never guess where I placed the loudspeakers…'

'As 13 is an unlucky number we raised
the strength of the Ministry to 31!'

'Full house, sir, but I'm afraid all of them are your cabinet
colleagues...'

'A poor view of the inauguration for
the public—but a good view of the
security men.'

'Just to unite the workers, I kept the
Namibia resolution for the
beginning...'

'Now go out there and shout: "We demand implementation of the recommendation for the modification of Section II in Para. 14.3 of Chapter IV of the M.P.C. Acts of 1955!"'

'Sensing our raw material problems the workers have threatened to withdraw their strike.'

'Unfortunately, the budget will benefit only the common man. We are not covered...'

"*I cannot give you a job but have corrected your application free of charge!*"

'*I thought you'd have become stone-hearted by now, hearing tales of woe like mine every day!*'

Flag Day

IF THEY CAN'T GET NEWSPRINT, LET THEM USE ART PAPER...

'You're confused, I'm not.'

RAVI SHANKAR

The Opposition is alive and well.

'We've already named the judge to conduct a probe into why the flag did not unfurl when you pulled the cord'.

... AND THIS, SIR, IS A WORKING MODEL!

The Raja of Ouch...

'What you need is just rest, hence,
you should join duty now ...'

'Who shall I say is crawling?'

'I see you now have a lady as the leader of the opposition. Stand up to her and don't be a coward as you are at home.'

'Mother-in-law and daughter-in-law have both won the Municipal elections, but from different parties. That's how the trouble has started.'

'Me CIA, and you?'

'What's wrong with my energy
programme? It's pure cowdung.'

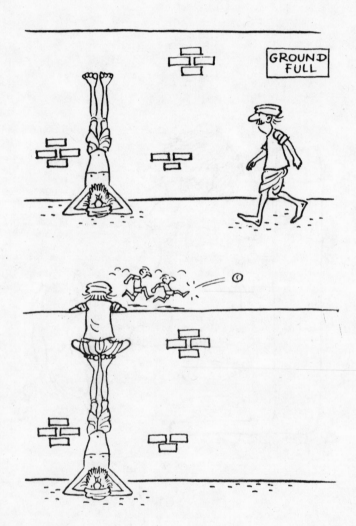

'Whatever we do, the Japanese always make it smaller, faster and cheaper.'

'Will the job involve a lot of paper work, sir?'

'*Me? I liked the book better.*'

'*Brothers, we must beware of aliens in our midst.*'

* Manu, the ancient/law-giver, gave caste legal sanction.

Mughal painting
circa 1981
Islamabad School

KUTTY

CROWN OF THORNS: Mr Mujibur Rahman is the "King" of Bangla Desh (29 Jan. 1975)

'Why are you sulking about not getting a transfer? Go
and beat up somebody, then you'll get it.'

Raja of Ouch...

'Before this I was plant manager and branch manager, and now, thanks to the corporate ladder...'

'Instead of a conveyance allowance, the company has agreed to give me a chiropodist allowance.'

'The operation is a success. The patient wants to know the latest score.'

'I spoke so convincingly that the audience turned off the mike, switched off the lights and fans and left the hall.'

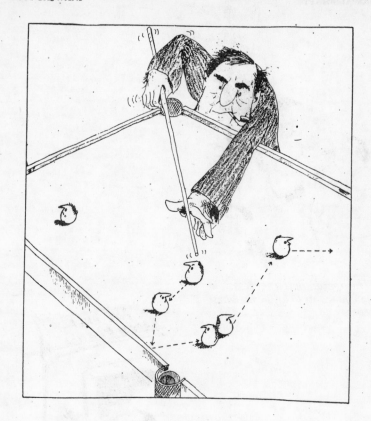

Breakfast TV

'My wife just refuses to let him go till our antenna is fixed.'

'That's why we came here.'

'Look, he didn't have the courtesy to invite me to his country.'

Mrs. Margaret Thatcher.

'No point wearing the halo—the days of ideology are over.'

BLACK MAN'S BURDEN

Star Warrior.

ABU

India exploded a nuclear device underground on 18 May 1974.

'This is your pilot speaking. We're about to land on earth. Please put on your oxygen masks!'

STRANGE, THE NEUTRON CIVILISATION—THEY WORSHIPPED PROPERTY!

Kapil Dev, cricketer.

RAJINI SHETTY

P.T. Usha, athlete.

Sunil Dutt, actor and
Member of Parliament.

A self portrait by G. Aravindan, distinguished Malayalam film director and cartoonist, and sketches of some characters from his new film, Oridathu.

Dr. S. Chandrasekhar, astro-physicist, winner of the 1983 Nobel Prize for Physics.

Double Talk ...

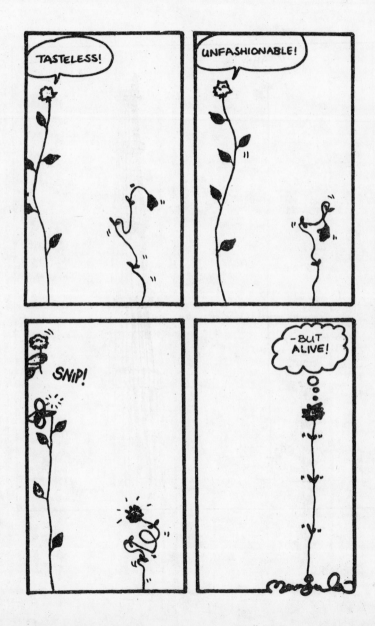

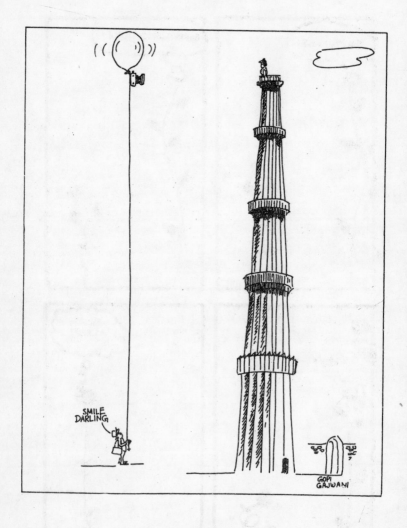

MORE ABOUT PENGUINS

For further information about books available from Penguins in India write to Penguin Books (India) Ltd, B4/246, Safdarjung Enclave, New Delhi 110 029.

In the UK: For a complete list of books available from Penguins in the United Kingdom write to Dept. EP, Penguin Books Ltd, Harmondsworth, Middlesex UB7 0DA.

In the U.S.A.: For a complete list of books available from Penguins in the United States write to Dept. DG, Penguin Books, 299 Murray Hill Parkway, East Rutherford, New Jersey 07073.

In Canada: For a complete list of books available from Penguins in Canada write to Penguin Books Canada Ltd, 2801 John Street, Markham, Ontario L3R 1B4.

In Australia: For a complete list of books available from Penguins in Australia write to the Marketing Department, Penguin Books Australia Ltd, P.O. Box 257, Ringwood, Victoria 3134.

In New Zealand: For a complete list of books available from Penguins in New Zealand write to the Marketing Department, Penguin Books (N.Z.) Ltd, Private Bag, Takapuna, Auckland 9.